# The Short Stories Of Bram Stoker

The short story is often viewed as an inferior relation to the Novel. But it is an art in itself. To take a story and distil its essence into fewer pages while keeping character and plot rounded and driven is not an easy task. Many try and many fail.

In this series we look at short stories from many of our most accomplished writers. Miniature masterpieces with a lot to say. In this volume we examine some of the short stories of Bram Stoker.

Born in November 1847 in Dublin, Ireland, Abraham Stoker was the third of seven children. Bed ridden with health issues until aged 7 he made a complete recovery on being sent to school. He was an excellent student excelling in maths and with a keen interest in Theatre.

He began his career as a theatre critic and after a favourable review was invited to meet the most important actor of the day, Henry Irving. They became great friends. After marriage to Florence Balcombe in 1878 they moved to London where he worked for Irving at his Lyceum theatre. It was here he started to write and then to travel extensively with Irving as he toured. Many of his novels are set from the places he visited though he never did go to Eastern Europe. He wrote many novels during his career but of course Dracula rises above all else.

In those last few moments drifting from wake to sleep we sometimes delve into thoughts of a very unpleasant kind. The hint of a shadow moving across the room can give rise to all sorts of troubling, unsettling ideas. Bram Stoker was a master of this effect. Who can forget the masterful creation of Dracula? Its realism built on diary entries, letters, newspapers clippings, ships log's was very clever and contributes to its lasting and pervading impact. Here, his sinister tales saturate your soul and hit your heart with untold fears that, layer by layer, reveal their true unutterable horror.

All of these stories are also available as an audiobook from our sister company Word Of Mouth. Many samples are at our youtube channel http://www.youtube.com/user/PortablePoetry?feature=mhee The full volume can be purchased from iTunes, Amazon and other digital stores. They are read for you by Richard Mitchley & Ghizela Rowe

**Index Of Stories**

The Judge's House

When the time for his examination drew near Malcolm Malcolmson made up his mind to go somewhere to read by himself. He feared the attractions of the seaside, and also he feared completely rural isolation, for of old he knew its charms, and so he determined to find some unpretentious little town where there would be nothing to distract him. He refrained from asking suggestions from any of his friends, for he argued that each would recommend some place of which he had knowledge, and where he had already acquaintances. As Malcolmson wished to avoid friends he had no wish to encumber himself with the attention of friends' friends and so he determined to look out for a place for himself. He packed a portmanteau with some clothes and all the books he required, and then took ticket for the first name on the local time-table which he did not know.

When at the end of three hours' journey he alighted at Benchurch, he felt satisfied that he had so far obliterated his tracks as to be sure of having a peaceful opportunity of pursuing his studies. He went straight to the one inn which the sleepy little place contained, and put up for the night. Benchurch was a market town, and once in three weeks was crowded to excess, but for the reminder of the twenty-one days it was as attractive as a desert. Malcolmson looked around the day after his arrival to try to find quarters more isolated than even so quiet an inn as "The Good Traveller" afforded. There was only one place which took his fancy, and it certainly satisfied his wildest ideas regarding quiet; in fact, quiet was not the proper word to apply to it - desolation was the only term conveying any suitable idea of its isolation. It was an old, rambling, heavy-built house of the Jacobean style, with heavy gables and windows, unusually small, and set higher than was customary in such houses, and was surrounded with a high brick wall massively built. Indeed, on examination, it looked more like a fortified house than an ordinary dwelling. But all these things pleased Malcolmson. "Here," he thought, "is the very spot I have been looking for, and if I can only get opportunity of using it I shall be happy." His joy was increased when he realized beyond doubt that it was not at present inhabited.

From the post-office he got the name of the agent, who was rarely surprised at the application to rent a part of the old house. Mr. Carnford, the local lawyer and agent, was a genial old gentleman, and frankly confessed his delight at anyone being willing to live in the house.

"To tell you the truth," said he, "I should be only too happy, on behalf of the owners, to let anyone have the house rent free, for a term of years if only to accustom the people here to see it inhabited. It has been so long empty that some kind of absurd prejudice has grown up about it, and this can be best put down by its occupation - if only," he added with a sly glance at Malcolmson, "by a scholar like yourself, who wants its quiet for a time."

Malcolmson thought it needless to ask the agent about the "absurd prejudice"; he knew he would get more information, if he should require it, on that subject from other quarters. He paid his three months' rent, got a receipt, and the name of an old woman who would probably undertake to "do" for him, and came away with the keys in his pocket. He then went to the landlady of the inn, who was a cheerful and most kindly person, and asked her advice as to such stores and provisions as he would be likely to require. She threw up her hands in amazement when he told her where he was going to settle himself.

"Not in the Judge's House!" she said, and grew pale as she spoke. He explained the locality of the house, saying that he did not know its name. When he had finished she answered:

"Aye, sure enough - sure enough the very place! It is the Judge's House sure enough." He asked her to tell him about the place, why so called, and what there was against it. She told him that it was so called locally because it had been many years before - how long she could not say, as she was herself from another part of the country, but she thought it must have been a hundred years or more - the abode of a judge who was held in great terror on account of his harsh sentences and his hostility to prisoners at Assizes. As to what there was against the house she could not tell. She had often asked, but no one could inform her, but there was a general feeling that there was something, and for her own part she would not take all the money in Drinkwater's Bank and stay in the house an hour by herself. Then she apologized to Malcolmson for her disturbing talk.

"It is too bad of me, sir, and you - and a young gentleman, too - if you will pardon me saying it, going to live there all alone. If you were my boy - and you'll excuse me for saying it - you wouldn't sleep there a night, not if I had to go there myself and pull the big alarm bell that's on the roof!" The good creature was so manifestly in earnest, and was so kindly in her intentions, that Malcolmson, although amused, was touched. He told her kindly how much he appreciated her interest in him, and added:

"But, my dear Mrs. Witham, indeed you need not be concerned about me! A man who is reading for the Mathematical Tripos has too much to think of to be disturbed by any of these mysterious 'somethings,' and his work is of too exact and prosaic a kind to allow of his having any order in his mind for mysteries of any kind. Harmonical Progression, Permutations and Combinations, and Elliptic Functions have sufficient mysteries for me!" Mrs. Witham kindly undertook to see after his commissions, and he went himself to look for the old woman who had been recommended to him. When he turned to the Judge's House with her, after an interval of a couple of hours, he found Mrs. Witham herself waiting with several men and boys carrying parcels, and an upholsterer's man with a bed in a cart, for she said, though table and chairs might be all very well, a bed that hadn't been aired for maybe fifty years was not proper for young ones to lie on. She was evidently curious to see the inside of the house, and though manifestly so afraid of the 'somethings' that at the slightest sound she clutched on to Malcolmson, whom she never left for a moment, went over the whole place.

After his examination of the house, Malcolmson decided to take up his abode in the great dining-room, which was big enough to serve for all his requirements, and Mrs. Witham, with the aid of the charwoman, Mrs. Dempster, proceeded to arrange matters. When the hampers were brought in and unpacked, Malcolmson saw that with much kind forethought she had sent from her own kitchen sufficient provisions to last for a few days. Before going she expressed all sorts of kind wishes, and at the door turned and said:

"And perhaps, sir, as the room is big and draughty it might be well to have one of those big screens put round your bed at night - though truth to tell, I would die myself if I were to be so shut in with all kinds of - of 'things,' that put their heads round the sides or over the top, and look on me!" The image which she had called up was too much for her nerves and she fled incontinently.

Mrs. Dempster sniffed in a superior manner as the landlady disappeared, and remarked that for her own part she wasn't afraid of all the bogies in the kingdom.

"I'll tell you what it is, sir," she said, "bogies is all kinds and sorts of things - except bogies! Rats and mice, and beetles and creaky doors, and loose slates, and broken panes, and stiff drawer handles, that stay out when you pull them and then fall down in the middle of the night. Look at the wainscot of the room! It is old - hundreds of years old! Do you think there's no rats and beetles there? And do you imagine, sir, that you won't see none of them? Rats is bogies, I tell you, and bogies is rats, and don't you get to think anything else!"

"Mrs. Dempster," said Malcolmson gravely, making her a polite bow, "you know more than a Senior Wrangler! And let me say that, as a mark of esteem for your indubitable soundness of head and heart, I shall, when I go, give you possession of this house, and let you stay here by yourself for the last two months of my tenancy, for four weeks will serve my purpose."

"Thank you kindly, sir!" she answered, "but I couldn't sleep away from home a night. I am in Greenhow's Charity, and if I slept a night away from my rooms I should lose all I have got to live on. The rules is very strict, and there's too many watching for a vacancy for me to run any risks in the matter. Only for that, sir, I'd gladly come here and attend on you altogether during your stay."

"My good woman," said Malcolmson hastily, "I have come here on a purpose to obtain solitude, and believe me that I am grateful to the late Greenhow for having organized his admirable charity - whatever it is - that I am perforce denied the opportunity of suffering from such a form of temptation! Saint Anthony himself could not be more rigid on the point!"

The old woman laughed harshly. "Ah, you young gentlemen," she said, "you don't fear for nought, and belike you'll get all the solitude you want here." She set to work with her cleaning, and by nightfall, when Malcolmson returned from his walk - he always had one of his books to study as he walked - he found the room swept and tidied, a fire burning on the old hearth, the lamp lit, and the table spread for supper with Mrs. Witham's excellent fare. "This is comfort indeed," he said, and rubbed his hands.

When he had finished his supper, and lifted the tray to the other end of the great oak dining-table, he got out his books again, put fresh wood on the fire, trimmed his lamp, and set himself down to a spell of real hard work. He went on without a pause till about eleven o'clock, when he knocked off for a bit to fix his fire and lamp, and to make himself a cup of tea. He had always been a tea-drinker, and during his college life had sat late at work and had taken tea late. The rest was a great luxury to him, and he enjoyed it with a sense of delicious voluptuous ease. The renewed fire leaped and sparkled, and threw quaint shadows through the great old room, and as he sipped his hot tea he revelled in the sense of isolation from his kind. Then it was that he began to notice for the first time what a noise the rats were making.

"Surely," he thought, "they cannot have been at it all the time I was reading. Had they been, I must have noticed it!" Presently, when the noise increased, he satisfied himself that it was really new. It was evident that at first the rats had been frightened at the presence of a stranger, and the light of fire and lamp, but that as the time went on they had grown bolder and were now disporting themselves as was their wont.

How busy they were - and hark to the strange noises! Up and down the old wainscot, over the ceiling and under the floor they raced, and gnawed, and scratched! Malcolmson smiled to himself as he recalled to mind the saying of Mrs. Dempster, "Bogies is rats, and rats is bogies!" The tea began to have its effect of intellectual and nervous stimulus, he saw with joy another long spell of work to be done before the night was past, and in the sense of security which it gave him, he allowed himself the luxury of a good look round the room. He took his lamp in one hand, and went all round, wondering that so quaint and beautiful an old house had been so long neglected. The carving of the oak on the panels of the wainscot was fine, and on and round the doors and windows it was beautiful and of rare merit. There were some old pictures on the walls, but they were coated so thick with dust and dirt that he could not distinguish any detail of them, though he held his lamp as high as he could over his head. Here and there as he went round he saw some crack or hole blocked for a moment by the face of a rat with its bright eyes glittering in the light, but in an instant it was gone, and a squeak and a scamper followed. The thing that most struck him, however, was the rope of the great alarm bell on the roof, which hung down in a corner of the room on the right-hand side of the fireplace. He pulled up close to the hearth a great high-backed carved oak chair, and sat down to his last cup of tea. When this was done he made up the fire, and went back to his work, sitting at the corner of the table, having the fire to his left. For a little while the rats disturbed him somewhat with their perpetual scampering, but he got accustomed to the noise as one does to the ticking of the clock or to the roar of moving water, and he became so immersed in his work that everything in the world, except the problem which he was trying to solve, passed away from him.

He suddenly looked up, his problem was still unsolved, and there was in the air that sense of the hour before the dawn, which is so dread to doubtful life. The noise of the rats had ceased. Indeed it seemed to him that it must have ceased but lately and that it was the sudden cessation which had disturbed him. The fire had fallen low, but still it threw out a deep red glow. As he looked he started in spite of his sang froid.

There, on the great high-backed carved oak chair by the right side of the fire-place sat an enormous rat, steadily glaring at him with baleful eyes. He made a motion to it as though to hunt it away, but it did not stir. Then he made the motion of throwing something. Still it did not stir, but showed its great white teeth angrily, and its cruel eyes shone in the lamplight with an added vindictiveness.

Malcolmson felt amazed, and seizing the poker from the hearth ran at it to kill it. Before, however, he could strike it the rat, with a squeak that sounded like the concentration of hate, jumped upon the floor, and, running up the rope of the alarm bell, disappeared in the darkness beyond the range of the green-shaded lamp. Instantly, strange to say, the noisy scampering of the rats in the wainscot began again.

By this time Malcolmson's mind was quite off the problem, and as a shrill cock-crow outside told him of the approach of morning, he went to bed and to sleep.

He slept so sound that he was not even waked by Mrs. Dempster coming in to make up his room. It was only when she had tided up the place and got his breakfast ready and tapped on the screen which closed in his bed that he woke. He was a little tired still after his night's hard work, but a strong cup of tea soon freshened him up and, taking his book, he went out for his morning walk, bringing with him a few sandwiches lest he should not care to return till dinner-time. He found a quiet walk between high elms some way outside the town, and here he spent the greater part of the day studying his Laplace. On his return he looked in to see Mrs. Witham and to thank her for her kindness. When she saw him coming through the diamond-paned bay window of her sanctum she came out to meet him and asked him in. She looked at him searchingly and shook her head as she said:

"You must not overdo it, sir. You are paler this morning than you should be. Too late hours and too hard work on the brains isn't good for any man! But tell me, sir, how did you pass the night? Well, I hope? But, my heart! sir, I was glad when Mrs. Dempster told me this morning that you were all right and sleeping sound when she went in." "Oh, I was all right," he answered smiling, "The 'somethings' didn't worry me, as yet. Only the rats, and they had a circus, I tell you, all over the place. There was one wicked-looking old devil that sat up on my own chair by the fire, and wouldn't go till I took the poker to him, and then he ran up the rope of the alarm bell and got to somewhere up the wall or the ceiling - I couldn't see where, it was so dark."

"Mercy on us," said Mrs. Witham, "an old devil, and sitting on a chair by the fireside! Take care, sir! take care! There's many a true word spoken in jest."

"How do you mean? 'Pon my word, I don't understand."

"An old devil! The old devil, perhaps. There! sir, you needn't laugh," for Malcolmson had broken into a hearty peal. "You young folks think it easy to laugh at things that makes older ones shudder. Never mind, sir! never mind! Please God, you'll laugh all the time. It's what I wish you myself!" and the good lady beamed all over in sympathy with his enjoyment, her fears gone for a moment.

"Oh, forgive me," said Malcolmson presently. "Don't think me rude, but the idea was too much for me - that the old devil himself was on the chair last night!" And at the thought he laughed again. Then he went home to dinner.

This evening the scampering of the rats began earlier, indeed it had been going on before his arrival, and only ceased whilst his presence by its freshness disturbed them. After dinner he sat by the fire for a while and had a smoke, and then, having cleared his table, began to work as before. To-night the rats disturbed him more than they had done on the previous night.

How they scampered up and down and under and over! How they squeaked and scratched and gnawed! How they, getting bolder by degrees, came to the mouths of their holes and to the chinks and cracks and crannies in the wainscoting till their eyes shone like tiny lamps as the firelight rose and fell. But to him, now doubtless accustomed to them, their eyes were not wicked, only their playfulness touched him. Sometimes the boldest of them made sallies out on the floor or along the mouldings of the wainscot. Now and again as they disturbed him Malcolmson made a sound to frighten them, smiting the table with his hand or giving a fierce "Hsh, hsh," so that they fled straightway to their holes.

And so the early part of the night wore on, and despite the noise Malcolmson got more and more immersed in his work.

All at once he stopped, as on the previous night, being overcome by a sudden silence. There was not the faintest sound of gnaw, or scratch, or squeak. The silence was as of the grave.

He remembered the odd occurrence of the previous night, and instinctively he looked at the chair standing close by the fireside. And then a very odd sensation thrilled through him.

There, on the great old high-backed carved oak chair beside the fireplace sat the same enormous rat, steadily glaring at him with baleful eyes.

Instinctively he took the nearest thing to his hand, a book of logarithms, and flung it at it. The book was badly aimed and the rat did not stir, so again the poker performance of the previous night was repeated, and again the rat, being closely pursued, fled up the rope of the alarm bell. Strangely, too, the departure of this rat was instantly followed by the renewal of the noise made by the general rat community. On this occasion, as on the previous one, Malcolmson could not see at what part of the room the rat disappeared, for the green shade of his lamp left the upper part of the room in darkness and the fire had burned low.

On looking at his watch he found it was close on midnight, and, not sorry for the divertissement, he made up his fire and made himself his nightly pot of tea. He had got through a good spell of work, and thought himself entitled to a cigarette, and so he sat on the great carved oak chair before the fire and enjoyed it. Whilst smoking he began to think that he would like to know where the rat disappeared to, for he had certain ideas for the morrow not entirely disconnected with a rat-trap. Accordingly he lit another lamp and placed it so that it would shine well into the right-hand corner of the wall by the fireplace. Then he got all the books he had with him, and placed them handy to throw at the vermin. Finally he lifted the rope of the alarm bell and placed the end of it on the table, fixing the extreme end under the lamp. As he handled it he could not help noticing how pliable it was, especially for so strong a rope and one not in use. "You could hang a man with it," he thought to himself. When his preparations were made he looked around, and said complacently:

"There now, my friend, I think we shall learn something of you this time!" He began his work again, and though, as before, somewhat disturbed at first by the noise of the rats, soon lost himself in his proposition and problems.

Again he was called to his immediate surroundings suddenly. This time it might not have been the sudden silence only which took his attention; there was a slight movement of the rope, and the lamp moved. Without stirring, he looked to see if his pile of books was within range, and then cast his eye along the rope. As he looked he saw the great rat drop from the rope on the oak arm-chair and sit there glaring at him. He raised a book in his right hand, and taking careful aim, flung it at the rat. The latter, with a quick movement, sprang aside and dodged the missile. Then he took another book, and a third, and flung them one after the other at the rat, but each time unsuccessfully. At last, as he stood with a book poised in his hand to throw, the rat squeaked and seemed afraid. This made Malcolmson more than ever eager to strike, and the book flew and struck the rat a resounding blow. It gave a terrified squeak, and turning on his pursuer a look of terrible malevolence, ran up the chair- back and made a great jump to the rope of the alarm bell and ran up it like lightning. The lamp rocked under the sudden strain, but it was a heavy one and did not topple over. Malcolmson kept his eyes on the rat, and saw it by the light of the second lamp leap to a moulding of the wainscot and disappear through a hole in one of the great pictures which hung on the wall, obscured and invisible through its coating of dirt and dust.

"I shall look up my friend's habitation in the morning," said the student, as he went over to collect his books. "The third picture from the fireplace, I shall not forget." He picked up the books one by one, commenting on them as he lifted them. Conic Sections he does not mind, nor Cycloid Oscillations, nor the Principia, nor Quaternions, nor Thermodynamics. Now for a look at the book that fetched him!" Malcolmson took it up and looked at it. As he did so he started, and a sudden pallor overspread his face. He looked round uneasily and shivered slightly, as he murmured to himself:

"The Bible my mother gave me! What an odd coincidence." He sat down to work again, and the rats in the wainscot renewed their gambols. They did not disturb him, however; somehow their presence gave him a sense of companionship. But he could not attend to his work, and after striving to master the subject on which he was engaged gave it up in despair, and went to bed as the first streak of dawn stole in through the eastern window.

He slept heavily but uneasily, and dreamed much, and when Mrs. Dempster woke him late in the morning he seemed ill at ease, and for a few minutes did not seem to realize exactly where he was. His first request rather surprised the servant.

"Mrs. Dempster, when I am out to-day I wish you would get the steps and dust or wash those pictures - specially that one the third from the fireplace - I want to see what they are."

Late in the afternoon Malcolmson worked at his books in the shaded walk, and the cheerfulness of the previous day came back to him as the day wore on, and he found that his reading was progressing well. He had worked out to a satisfactory conclusion all the problems which had as yet baffled him, and it was in a state of jubilation that he paid a visit to Mrs. Witham at "The Good Traveller." He found a stranger in the cosy sitting-room with the landlady, who was introduced to him as Dr. Thornhill. She was not quite at ease, and this, combined with the doctor's plunging at once into a series of questions, made Malcolmson come to the conclusion that his presence was not an accident, so without preliminary he said:

"Dr. Thornhill, I shall with pleasure answer you any question you may choose to ask me if you will answer me one question first."

The doctor seemed surprised, but he smiled and answered at once, "Done! What is it?"

"Did Mrs. Witham ask you to come here and see me and advise me?"

Dr. Thornhill for a moment was taken aback, and Mrs. Witham got fiery red and turned away, but the doctor was a frank and ready man, and he answered at once and openly:

"She did, but she didn't intend you to know it. I suppose it was my clumsy haste that made you suspect. She told me that she did not like the idea of your being in that house all by yourself, and that she thought you took too much strong tea. In fact, she wants me to advise you, if possible, to give up the tea and the very late hours. I was a keen student in my time, so I suppose I may take the liberty of a college man, and without offence, advise you not quite as a stranger."

Malcolmson with a bright smile held out his hand. "Shake - as they say in America," he said. "I must thank you for your kindness, and Mrs. Witham too, and your kindness deserves a return on my part. I promise to take no more strong tea - no tea at all till you let me - and I shall go to bed to-night at one o'clock at latest. Will that do?"

"Capital," said the doctor. "Now tell us all that you noticed in the old house," and so Malcolmson then and there told in minute detail all that had happened in the last two nights. He was interrupted every now and then by some exclamation from Mrs. Witham, till finally when he told of the episode of the Bible the landlady's pent-up emotions found vent in a shriek, and it was not till a stiff glass of brandy and water had been administered that she grew composed again. Dr. Thornhill listened with a face of growing gravity, and when the narrative was complete and Mrs. Witham had been restored he asked:

"The rat always went up the rope of the alarm bell?"

"Always."

"I suppose you know," said the Doctor after a pause, "what that rope is?"

"No?"

"It is," said the Doctor slowly, "the very rope which the hangman used for all the victims of the Judge's judicial rancour!" Here he was interrupted by another scream from Mrs. Witham, and steps had to be taken for her recovery. Malcolmson having looked at his watch, and found that it was close to his dinner-hour, had gone home before her complete recovery.

When Mrs. Witham was herself again she almost assailed the Doctor with angry questions as to what he meant by putting such horrible ideas into the poor young man's mind. "He has quite enough there already to upset him," she added.

Dr. Thornhill replied:

"My dear madam, I had a distinct purpose in it! I wanted to draw his attention to the bell-rope, and to fix it there. It may be that he is in a highly over-wrought state, and has been studying too much, although I am bound to say that he seems as sound and healthy a young man, mentally and bodily, as ever I saw - but then the rats - and that suggestion of the devil." The doctor shook his head and went on. "I would have offered to go and stay the first night with him but that I felt sure it would have been a cause of offence. He may get in the night some strange fright or hallucination, and if he does I want him to pull that rope. All alone as he is it will give us warning, and we may reach him in time to be of service. I shall be sitting up pretty late to-night and shall keep my ears open. Do not be alarmed if Benchurch gets a surprise before morning."

"Oh, Doctor, what do you mean? What do you mean?"

"I mean this, that possibly - nay, more probably - we shall hear the great alarm-bell from the Judge's House to-night," and the Doctor made about an effective an exit as could be thought of.

When Malcolmson arrived home he found that it was a little after his usual time, and Mrs. Dempster had gone away - the rules of Greenhow's Charity were not to be neglected. He was glad to see that the place was bright and tidy with a cheerful fire and a well-trimmed lamp. The evening was colder than might have been expected in April, and a heavy wind was blowing with such rapidly-increasing strength that there was every promise of a storm during the night. For a few minutes after his entrance the noise of the rats ceased, but so soon as they became accustomed to his presence they began again. He was glad to hear them, for he felt once more the feeling of companionship in their noise, and his mind ran back to the strange fact that they only ceased to manifest themselves when the other - the great rat with the baleful eyes - came upon the scene. The reading- lamp only was lit and its green shade kept the ceiling and the upper part of the room in darkness so that the cheerful light from the hearth spreading over the floor and shining on the white cloth laid over the end of the table was warm and cheery. Malcolmson sat down to his dinner with a good appetite and a buoyant spirit. After his dinner and a cigarette he sat steadily down to work, determined not to let anything disturb him, for he remembered his promise to the doctor, and made up his mind to make the best of the time at his disposal.

For an hour or so he worked all right, and then his thoughts began to wander from his books. The actual circumstances around him, and the calls on his physical attention, and his nervous susceptibility were not to be denied. By this time the wind had become a gale, and the gale a storm. The old house, solid though it was, seemed to shake to its foundation, and the storm roared and raged through its many chimneys and its queer old gables, producing strange, unearthly sounds in the empty rooms and corridors. Even the great alarm-bell on the roof must have felt the force of the wind, for the rope rose and fell slightly, as though the bell were moved a little from time to time, and the limber rope fell on the oak floor with a hard and hollow sound.

As Malcolmson listened to it he bethought himself of the doctor's words, "It is the rope which the hangman used for the victims of the Judge's judicial rancour," and he went over to the corner of the fireplace and took it in his hand to look at it. There seemed a sort of deadly interest in it, and as he stood there he lost himself for a moment in speculation as to who these victims were, and the grim wish of the Judge to have such a ghastly relic ever under his eyes. As he stood there the swaying of the bell on the roof still lifted the rope now and again, but presently there came a new sensation - a sort of tremor in the rope, as though something was moving along it.

Looking up instinctively Malcolmson saw the great rat coming slowly down towards him, glaring at him steadily. He dropped the rope and started back with a muttered curse, and the rat turning ran up the slope again and disappeared, and at the same instant Malcolmson became conscious that the noise of the other rats, which had ceased for a while, began again.

All this set him thinking, and it occurred to him that he had not investigated the lair of the rat or looked at the pictures, as he had intended. He lit the other lamp without the shade, and, holding it up went and stood opposite the third picture from the fireplace on the right-hand side where he had seen the rat disappear on the previous night.

At the first glance he started back so suddenly that he almost dropped the lamp, and a deadly pallor overspread his face.

His knees shook, and heavy drops of sweat came on his forehead, and he trembled like an aspen. But he was young and plucky, and pulled himself together, and after the pause of a few seconds stepped forward again, raised the lamp, and examined the picture which had been dusted and washed, and now stood out clearly.

It was of a judge dressed in his robes of scarlet and ermine. His face was strong and merciless, evil, crafty and vindictive, with a sensual mouth, hooked nose of ruddy colour, and shaped like the beak of a bird of prey. The rest of the face was of a cadaverous colour. The eyes were of peculiar brilliance and with a terribly malignant expression. As he looked at them, Malcolmson grew cold, for he saw there the very counterpart of the eyes of the great rat. The lamp almost fell from his hand, he saw the rat with its baleful eyes peering out through the hole in the corner of the picture, and noted the sudden cessation of the noise of the other rats. However, he pulled himself together, and went on with his examination of the picture.

The Judge was seated in a great high-backed carved oak chair, on the right-hand side of a great stone fireplace where, in the corner, a rope hung down from the ceiling, its end lying coiled on the floor. With a feeling of something like horror, Malcolmson recognized the scene of the room as it stood, and gazed around him in an awestruck manner as though he expected to find some strange presence behind him. Then he looked over to the corner of the fireplace - and with a loud cry he let the lamp fall from his hand.

There, in the judge's arm-chair, with the rope hanging behind, sat the rat with the Judge's baleful eyes, now intensified as with a fiendish leer. Save for the howling of the storm without there was silence.

The fallen lamp recalled Malcolmson to himself. Fortunately it was of metal, and so the oil was not spilt. However, the practical need of attending to it settled at once his nervous apprehensions. When he had turned it out, he wiped his brow and thought for a moment.

"This will not do," he said to himself. "If I go on like this I shall become a crazy fool. This must stop! I promised the doctor I would not take tea. Faith, he was pretty right! My nerves must have been getting into a queer state. Funny I did not notice it. I never felt better in my life. However, it is all right now, and I shall not be such a fool again."

Then he mixed himself a good stiff glass of brandy and water and resolutely sat down to his work.

It was nearly an hour when he looked up from his book, disturbed by the sudden stillness. Without, the wind howled and roared louder then ever, and the rain drove in sheets against the windows, beating like hail on the glass, but within there was no sound whatever save the echo of the wind as it roared in the great chimney, and now and then a hiss as a few raindrops found their way down the chimney in a lull of the storm. The fire had fallen low and had ceased to flame, though it threw out a red glow. Malcolmson listened attentively, and presently heard a thin, squeaking noise, very faint. It came from the corner of the room where the rope hung down, and he thought it was the creaking of the rope on the floor as the swaying of the bell raised and lowered it. Looking up, however, he saw in the dim light the great rat clinging to the rope and gnawing it. The rope was already nearly gnawed through - he could see the lighter colour where the strands were laid bare. As he looked the job was completed, and the severed end of the rope fell clattering on the oaken floor, whilst for an instant the great rat remained like a knob or tassel at the end of the rope, which now began to sway to and fro. Malcolmson felt for a moment another pang of terror as he thought that now the possibility of calling the outer world to his assistance was cut off, but an intense anger took its place, and seizing the book he was reading he hurled it at the rat. The blow was well-aimed, but before the missile could reach him the rat dropped off and struck the floor with a soft thud. Malcolmson instantly rushed over towards him, but it darted away and disappeared in the darkness of the shadows of the room. Malcolmson felt that his work was over for the night, and determined then and there to vary the monotony of the proceedings by a hunt for the rat, and took off the green shade of the lamp so as to insure a wider spreading light. As he did so the gloom of the upper part of the room was relieved, and in the new flood of light, great by comparison with the previous darkness, the pictures on the wall stood out boldly.

From where he stood, Malcolmson saw right opposite to him the third picture on the wall from the right of the fireplace. He rubbed his eyes in surprise, and then a great fear began to come upon him.

In the centre of the picture was a great irregular patch of brown canvas, as fresh as when it was stretched on the frame. The background was as before, with chair and chimney-corner and rope, but the figure of the Judge had disappeared.

Malcolmson, almost in a chill of horror, turned slowly round, and then he began to shake and tremble like a man in a palsy. His strength seemed to have left him, and he was incapable of action or movement, hardly even of thought. He could only see and hear.

There, on the great high-backed carved oak chair sat the judge in his robes of scarlet and ermine, with his baleful eyes glaring vindictively, and a smile of triumph on the resolute cruel mouth, as he lifted with his hands a black cap. Malcolmson felt as if the blood was running from his heart, as one does in moments of prolonged suspense. There was a singing in his ears. Without, he could hear the roar and howl of the tempest, and through it, swept on the storm, came the striking of midnight by the great chimes in the market-place. He stood for a space of time that seemed to him endless still as a statue, and with wide-open, horror-struck eyes, breathless. As the clock struck, so the smile of triumph on the Judge's face intensified, and at the last stroke of midnight he placed the black cap on his head.

Slowly and deliberately the Judge rose from his chair and picked up the piece of rope of the alarm bell which lay on the floor, drew it through his hands as if he enjoyed its touch and then deliberately began to knot one end of it, fashioning it into a noose. This he tightened and tested with his foot, pulling hard at it till he was satisfied and then making a running noose of it, which he held in his hand. Then he began to move along the table on the opposite side of Malcolmson keeping his eyes on him until he had passed him, when with a quick movement he stood in front of the door. Malcolmson then began to feel that he was trapped, and tried to think of what he should do. There was some fascination in the Judge's eyes, which he never took off him, and he had, perforce, to look. He saw the Judge approach - still keeping between him and the door - and raise the noose and throw it towards him as if to entangle him. With a great effort he made a quick movement to one side, and saw the rope fall beside him, and heard it strike the oaken floor. Again the Judge raised the noose and tried to ensnare him, ever keeping his baleful eyes fixed on him, and each time by a mighty effort the student just managed to evade it. So this went on for many times, the Judge seeming never discouraged nor discomposed at failure, but playing as a cat does with a mouse. At last in despair, which had reached its climax, Malcolmson cast a quick glance round him. The lamp seemed to have blazed up, and there was a fairly good light in the room. At the many rat-holes and in the chinks and crannies of the wainscot he saw the rats' eyes, and this aspect, that was purely physical, gave him a gleam of comfort. He looked round and saw that the rope of the great alarm bell was laden with rats. Every inch of it was covered with them, and more and more were pouring through the small circular hole in the ceiling whence it emerged, so that with their weight the bell was beginning to sway.

Hark! it had swayed till the clapper had touched the bell. The sound was but a tiny one, but the bell was only beginning to sway, and it would increase.

At the sound the Judge, who had been keeping his eyes fixed on Malcolmson, looked up, and a scowl of diabolical anger overspread his face. His eyes fairly glowed like hot coals, and he stamped his foot with a sound that seemed to make the house shake. A dreadful peal of thunder broke overhead as he raised the rope again, whilst the rats kept running up and down the rope as though working against time. This time, instead of throwing it, he drew close to his victim, and held open the noose as he approached. As he came closer there seemed something paralyzing in his very presence, and Malcolmson stood rigid as a corpse. He felt the Judge's icy fingers touch his throat as he adjusted the rope. The noose tightened - tightened. Then the Judge, taking the rigid form of the student in his arms, carried him over and placed him standing in the oak chair, and stepping up beside him, put his hand up and caught the end of the swaying rope of the alarm-bell. As he raised his hand the rats fled squeaking and disappeared through the hole in the ceiling. Taking the end of the noose which was round Malcolmson's neck he tied it to the hanging bell-rope, and then descending pulled away the chair.

When the alarm-bell of the Judge's House began to sound a crowd soon assembled. Lights and torches of various kinds appeared, and soon a silent crowd was hurrying to the spot. They knocked loudly at the door, but there was no reply. Then they burst in the door, and poured into the great dining-room, the doctor at the head.

There at the end of the rope of the great alarm-bell hung the body of the student, and on the face of the Judge in the picture was a malignant smile.


Dracula's Guest

Dracula's Guest was excised from the original Dracula manuscript by its publisher because of the length of the original book.  It was published as a short story in 1914, two years after Stoker's death.


When we started for our drive the sun was shining brightly on Munich, and the air was full of the joyousness of early summer.

Just as we were about to depart, Herr Delbruck (the maitre d'hotel of the Quatre Saisons, where I was staying) came down bareheaded to the carriage and, after wishing me a pleasant drive, said to the coachman, still holding his hand on the handle of the carriage door, "Remember you are back by nightfall.  The sky looks bright but there is a shiver in the north wind that says there may be a sudden storm.

But I am sure you will not be late."  Here he smiled and added, "for you know what night it is."

Johann answered with an emphatic, "Ja, mein Herr," and, touching his hat, drove off quickly. When we had cleared the town, I said, after signalling to him to stop:

"Tell me, Johann, what is tonight?"

He crossed himself, as he answered laconically: "Walpurgis nacht."

Then he took out his watch, a great, old-fashioned German silver thing as big as a turnip and looked at it, with his eyebrows gathered together and a little impatient shrug of his shoulders. I realized that this was his way of respectfully protesting against the unnecessary delay and sank back in the carriage, merely motioning him to proceed. He started off rapidly, as if to make up for lost time. Every now and then the horses seemed to throw up their heads and sniff the air suspiciously. On such occasions I often looked round in alarm. The road was pretty bleak, for we were traversing a sort of high windswept plateau. As we drove, I saw a road that looked but little used and which seemed to dip through a little winding valley.

It looked so inviting that, even at the risk of offending him, I called Johann to stop and when he had pulled up, I told him I would like to drive down that road. He made all sorts of excuses and frequently crossed himself as he spoke. This somewhat piqued my curiosity, so I asked him various questions. He answered fencingly and repeatedly looked at his watch in protest.

Finally I said, "Well, Johann, I want to go down this road. I shall not ask you to come unless you like; but tell me why you do not like to go, that is all I ask." For answer he seemed to throw himself off the box, so quickly did he reach the ground. Then he stretched out his hands appealingly to me and implored me not to go.

There was just enough of English mixed with the German for me to understand the drift of his talk. He seemed always just about to tell me something the very idea of which evidently frightened him; but each time he pulled himself up saying, "Walpurgis nacht!"

I tried to argue with him, but it was difficult to argue with a man when I did not know his language. The advantage certainly rested with him, for although he began to speak in English, of a very crude and broken kind, he always got excited and broke into his native tongue and every time he did so, he looked at his watch. Then the horses became restless and sniffed the air.

At this he grew very pale, and, looking around in a frightened way, he suddenly jumped forward, took them by the bridles, and led them on some twenty feet. I followed and asked why he had done this. For an answer he crossed himself, pointed to the spot we had left, and drew his carriage in the direction of the other road, indicating a cross, and said, first in German, then in English, "Buried him - him what killed themselves."

I remembered the old custom of burying suicides at cross roads: "Ah! I see, a suicide. How interesting!" But for the life of me I could not make out why the horses were frightened.

Whilst we were talking, we heard a sort of sound between a yelp and a bark.  It was far away; but the horses got very restless, and it took Johann all his time to quiet them.  He was pale and said, "It sounds like a wolf but yet there are no wolves here now."

"No?" I said, questioning him.  "Isn't it long since the wolves were so near the city?"

"Long, long," he answered, "in the spring and summer; but with the snow the wolves have been here not so long."

Whilst he was petting the horses and trying to quiet them, dark clouds drifted rapidly across the sky.  The sunshine passed away, and a breath of cold wind seemed to drift over us.  It was only a breath, however, and more of a warning than a fact, for the sun came out brightly again.

Johann looked under his lifted hand at the horizon and said, "The storm of snow, he comes before long time."  Then he looked at his watch again, and, straightway holding his reins firmly - for the horses were still pawing the ground restlessly and shaking their heads he climbed to his box as though the time had come for proceeding on our journey.

I felt a little obstinate and did not at once get into the carriage.

"Tell me," I said, "about this place where the road leads," and I pointed down.

Again he crossed himself and mumbled a prayer before he answered, "It is unholy."

"What is unholy?" I enquired.

"The village."

"Then there is a village?"

"No, no.  No one lives there hundreds of years."

My curiosity was piqued, "But you said there was a village."

"There was."

"Where is it now?"

Whereupon he burst out into a long story in German and English, so mixed up that I could not quite understand exactly what he said.

Roughly I gathered that long ago, hundreds of years, men had died there and been buried in their graves; but sounds were heard under the clay, and when the graves were opened, men and women were found rosy with life and their mouths red with blood.  And so, in haste to save their lives (aye, and their souls! Aand here he crossed himself) those who were left fled away to other places, where the living lived and the dead were dead and not - not something.  He was evidently afraid to speak the last words.  As he proceeded with his narration, he grew more and more excited.  It seemed as if his imagination had got hold of him, and he ended in a perfect paroxysm of fear-white-faced, perspiring, trembling, and looking round him as if expecting that some dreadful presence would manifest itself there in the bright sunshine on the open plain.

Finally, in an agony of desperation, he cried, "Walpurgis nacht!" and pointed to the carriage for me to get in.

All my English blood rose at this, and standing back I said, "You are afraid, Johann you are afraid.  Go home, I shall return alone, the walk will do me good." The carriage door was open.  I took from the seat my oak walking stick, which I always carry on my holiday excursions and closed the door, pointing back to Munich, and said, "Go home, Johann, Walpurgis nacht doesn't concern Englishmen."

The horses were now more restive than ever, and Johann was trying to hold them in, while excitedly imploring me not to do anything so foolish.  I pitied the poor fellow, he was so deeply in earnest; but all the same I could not help laughing.  His English was quite gone now.  In his anxiety he had forgotten that his only means of making me understand was to talk my language, so he jabbered away in his native German.  It began to be a little tedious.  After giving the direction, "Home!" I turned to go down the cross road into the valley.

With a despairing gesture, Johann turned his horses towards Munich.  I leaned on my stick and looked after him.  He went slowly along the road for a while, then there came over the crest of the hill a man tall and thin.  I could see so much in the distance.  When he drew near the horses, they began to jump and kick about, then to scream with terror.  Johann could not hold them in; they bolted down the road, running away madly.  I watched them out of sight, then looked for the stranger; but I found that he, too, was gone.

With a light heart I turned down the side road through the deepening valley to which Johann had objected.  There was not the slightest reason, that I could see, for his objection; and I daresay I tramped for a couple of hours without thinking of time or distance and certainly without seeing a person or a house. So far as the place was concerned, it was desolation itself.  But I did not notice this particularly till, on turning a bend in the road, I came upon a scattered fringe of wood; then I recognized that I had been impressed unconsciously by the desolation of the region through which I had passed.

I sat down to rest myself and began to look around.  It struck me that it was considerably colder than it had been at the commencement of my walk, a sort of sighing sound seemed to be around me with, now and then, high overhead, a sort of muffled roar.  Looking upwards I noticed that great thick clouds were drafting rapidly across the sky from north to south at a great height.  There were signs of a coming storm in some lofty stratum of the air.

I was a little chilly, and, thinking that it was the sitting still after the exercise of walking, I resumed my journey.

The ground I passed over was now much more picturesque. There were no striking objects that the eye might single out, but in all there was a charm of beauty. I took little heed of time, and it was only when the deepening twilight forced itself upon me that I began to think of how I should find my way home. The air was cold, and the drifting of clouds high overhead was more marked. They were accompanied by a sort of far away rushing sound, through which seemed to come at intervals that mysterious cry which the driver had said came from a wolf. For a while I hesitated. I had said I would see the deserted village, so on I went and presently came on a wide stretch of open country, shut in by hills all around. Their sides were covered with trees which spread down to the plain, dotting in clumps the gentler slopes and hollows which showed here and there. I followed with my eye the winding of the road and saw that it curved close to one of the densest of these clumps and was lost behind it.

As I looked there came a cold shiver in the air, and the snow began to fall. I thought of the miles and miles of bleak country I had passed, and then hurried on to seek shelter of the wood in front. Darker and darker grew the sky, and faster and heavier fell the snow, till the earth before and around me was a glistening white carpet the further edge of which was lost in misty vagueness.

The road was here but crude, and when on the level its boundaries were not so marked as when it passed through the cuttings; and in a little while I found that I must have strayed from it, for I missed underfoot the hard surface, and my feet sank deeper in the grass and moss. Then the wind grew stronger and blew with ever increasing force, till I was fain to run before it. The air became icy cold, and in spite of my exercise I began to suffer. The snow was now falling so thickly and whirling around me in such rapid eddies that I could hardly keep my eyes open. Every now and then the heavens were torn asunder by vivid lightning, and in the flashes I could see ahead of me a great mass of trees, chiefly yew and cypress all heavily coated with snow.

I was soon amongst the shelter of the trees, and there in comparative silence I could hear the rush of the wind high overhead. Presently the blackness of the storm had become merged in the darkness of the night. By-and-by the storm seemed to be passing away, it now only came in fierce puffs or blasts. At such moments the weird sound of the wolf appeared to be echoed by many similar sounds around me.

Now and again, through the black mass of drifting cloud, came a straggling ray of moonlight which lit up the expanse and showed me that I was at the edge of a dense mass of cypress and yew trees. As the snow had ceased to fall, I walked out from the shelter and began to investigate more closely. It appeared to me that, amongst so many old foundations as I had passed, there might be still standing a house in which, though in ruins, I could find some sort of shelter for a while. As I skirted the edge of the copse, I found that a low wall encircled it, and following this I presently found an opening. Here the cypresses formed an alley leading up to a square mass of some kind of building. Just as I caught sight of this, however, the drifting clouds obscured the moon, and I passed up the path in darkness.

The wind must have grown colder, for I felt myself shiver as I walked; but there was hope of shelter, and I groped my way blindly on.

I stopped, for there was a sudden stillness. The storm had passed; and, perhaps in sympathy with nature's silence, my heart seemed to cease to beat. But this was only momentarily; for suddenly the moonlight broke through the clouds showing me that I was in a graveyard and that the square object before me was a great massive tomb of marble, as white as the snow that lay on and all around it. With the moonlight there came a fierce sigh of the storm which appeared to resume its course with a long, low howl, as of many dogs or wolves. I was awed and shocked, and I felt the cold perceptibly grow upon me till it seemed to grip me by the heart. Then while the flood of moonlight still fell on the marble tomb, the storm gave further evidence of renewing, as though it were returning on its track. Impelled by some sort of fascination, I approached the sepulchre to see what it was and why such a thing stood alone in such a place. I walked around it and read, over the Doric door, in German:

COUNTESS DOLINGEN OF GRATZ
IN STYRIA
SOUGHT AND FOUND DEATH
1801

On the top of the tomb, seemingly driven through the solid marble - for the structure was composed of a few vast blocks of stone - was a great iron spike or stake. On going to the back I saw, graven in great Russian letters:

THE DEAD TRAVEL FAST.

There was something so weird and uncanny about the whole thing that it gave me a turn and made me feel quite faint. I began to wish, for the first time, that I had taken Johann's advice. Here a thought struck me, which came under almost myssterious circumstances and with a terrible shock. This was Walpurgis Night!

Walpurgis Night was when, according to the belief of millions of people, the devil was abroad; when the graves were opened and the dead came forth and walked. When all evil things of earth and air and water held revel. This very place the driver had specially shunned. This was the depopulated village of centuries ago. This was where the suicide lay; and this was the place where I was alone - unmanned, shivering with cold in a shroud of snow with a wild storm gathering again upon me! It took all my philosophy, all the religion I had been taught, all my courage, not to collapse in a paroxysm of fright.

And now a perfect tornado burst upon me. The ground shook as though thousands of horses thundered across it; and this time the storm bore on its icy wings, not snow, but great hailstones which drove with such violence that they might have come from the thongs of Balearic slingers--hailstones that beat down leaf and branch and made the shelter of the cypresses of no more avail than though their stems were standing corn. At the first I had rushed to the nearest tree; but I was soon fain to leave it and seek the only spot that seemed to afford refuge, the deep Doric doorway of the marble tomb.

There, crouching against the massive bronze door, I gained a certain amount of protection from the beating of the hailstones, for now they only drove against me as they ricochetted from the ground and the side of the marble.

As I leaned against the door, it moved slightly and opened inwards. The shelter of even a tomb was welcome in that pitiless tempest and I was about to enter it when there came a flash of forked lightning that lit up the whole expanse of the heavens. In the instant, as I am a living man, I saw, as my eyes turned into the darkness of the tomb, a beautiful woman with rounded cheeks and red lips, seemingly sleeping on a bier. As the thunder broke overhead, I was grasped as by the hand of a giant and hurled out into the storm.

The whole thing was so sudden that, before I could realize the shock, moral as well as physical, I found the hailstones beating me down. At the same time I had a strange, dominating feeling that I was not alone. I looked towards the tomb. Just then there came another blinding flash which seemed to strike the iron stake that surmounted the tomb and to pour through to the earth, blasting and crumbling the marble, as in a burst of flame. The dead woman rose for a moment of agony while she was lapped in the flame, and her bitter scream of pain was drowned in the thundercrash. The last thing I heard was this mingling of dreadful sound, as again I was seized in the giant grasp and dragged away, while the hailstones beat on me and the air around seemed reverberant with the howling of wolves. The last sight that I remembered was a vague, white, moving mass, as if all the graves around me had sent out the phantoms of their sheeted dead, and that they were closing in on me through the white cloudiness of the driving hail.

Gradually there came a sort of vague beginning of consciousness, then a sense of weariness that was dreadful. For a time I remembered nothing, but slowly my senses returned. My feet seemed positively racked with pain, yet I could not move them. They seemed to be numbed. There was an icy feeling at the back of my neck and all down my spine, and my ears, like my feet, were dead yet in torment; but there was in my breast a sense of warmth which was by comparison delicious. It was as a nightmare--a physical nightmare, if one may use such an expression; for some heavy weight on my chest made it difficult for me to breathe.

This period of semilethargy seemed to remain a long time, and as it faded away I must have slept or swooned. Then came a sort of loathing, like the first stage of seasickness, and a wild desire to be free of something - I knew not what. A vast stillness enveloped me, as though all the world were asleep or dead only broken by the low panting as of some animal close to me. I felt a warm rasping at my throat, then came a consciousness of the awful truth which chilled me to the heart and sent the blood surging up through my brain. Some great animal was lying on me and now licking my throat. I feared to stir, for some instinct of prudence bade me lie still; but the brute seemed to realize that there was now some change in me, for it raised its head. Through my eyelashes I saw above me the two great flaming eyes of a gigantic wolf. Its sharp white teeth gleamed in the gaping red mouth, and I could feel its hot breath fierce and acrid upon me.

For another spell of time I remembered no more.  Then I became conscious of a low growl, followed by a yelp, renewed again and again.  Then seemingly very far away, I heard a "Holloa! holloa!" as of many voices calling in unison.  Cautiously I raised my head and looked in the direction whence the sound came, but the cemetery blocked my view.

The wolf still continued to yelp in a strange way, and a red glare began to move round the grove of cypresses, as though following the sound.  As the voices drew closer, the wolf yelped faster and louder.  I feared to make either sound or motion.  Nearer came the red glow over the white pall which stretched into the darkness around me.  Then all at once from beyond the trees there came at a trot a troop of horsemen bearing torches.  The wolf rose from my breast and made for the cemetery.  I saw one of the horsemen (soldiers by their caps and their long military cloaks) raise his carbine and take aim.  A companion knocked up his arm, and I heard the ball whiz over my head.  He had evidently taken my body for that of the wolf. Another sighted the animal as it slunk away, and a shot followed.  Then, at a gallop, the troop rode forward, some towards me, others following the wolf as it disappeared amongst the snow-clad cypresses.

As they drew nearer I tried to move but was powerless, although I could see and hear all that went on around me.  Two or three of the soldiers jumped from their horses and knelt beside me.  One of them raised my head and placed his hand over my heart.

"Good news, comrades!" he cried.  "His heart still beats!"

Then some brandy was poured down my throat; it put vigor into me, and I was able to open my eyes fully and look around.  Lights and shadows were moving among the trees, and I heard men call to one another.  They drew together, uttering frightened exclamations; and the lights flashed as the others came pouring out of the cemetery pell-mell, like men possessed.  When the further ones came close to us, those who were around me asked them eagerly, "Well, have you found him?"

The reply rang out hurriedly, "No! no!  Come away quick, quick! This is no place to stay, and on this of all nights!"

"What was it?" was the question, asked in all manner of keys.  The answer came variously and all indefinitely as though the men were moved by some common impulse to speak yet were restrained by some common fear from giving their thoughts.

"It-it-indeed!" gibbered one, whose wits had plainly given out for the moment.

"A wolf and yet not a wolf!" another put in shudderingly.

"No use trying for him without the sacred bullet," a third remarked in a more ordinary manner.

"Serve us right for coming out on this night!  Truly we have earned our thousand marks!" were the ejaculations of a fourth.

"There was blood on the broken marble," another said after a pause, "the lightning never brought that there. And for him - is he safe? Look at his throat! See comrades, the wolf has been lying on him and keeping his blood warm."

The officer looked at my throat and replied, "He is all right, the skin is not pierced. What does it all mean? We should never have found him but for the yelping of the wolf."

"What became of it?" asked the man who was holding up my head and who seemed the least panic-stricken of the party, for his hands were steady and without tremor.

On his sleeve was the chevron of a petty officer.

"It went home," answered the man, whose long face was pallid and who actually shook with terror as he glanced around him fearfully. "There are graves enough there in which it may lie. Come, comrades, come quickly! Let us leave this cursed spot."

The officer raised me to a sitting posture, as he uttered a word of command; then several men placed me upon a horse. He sprang to the saddle behind me, took me in his arms, gave the word to advance; and, turning our faces away from the cypresses, we rode away in swift military order.

As yet my tongue refused its office, and I was perforce silent. I must have fallen asleep; for the next thing I remembered was finding myself standing up, supported by a soldier on each side of me. It was almost broad daylight, and to the north a red streak of sunlight was reflected like a path of blood over the waste of snow.

The officer was telling the men to say nothing of what they had seen, except that they found an English stranger, guarded by a large dog.

"Dog! that was no dog," cut in the man who had exhibited such fear. "I think I know a wolf when I see one."

The young officer answered calmly, "I said a dog."

"Dog!" reiterated the other ironically. It was evident that his courage was rising with the sun; and, pointing to me, he said, "Look at his throat. Is that the work of a dog, master?"

Instinctively I raised my hand to my throat, and as I touched it I cried out in pain. The men crowded round to look, some stooping down from their saddles; and again there came the calm voice of the young officer, "A dog, as I said. If aught else were said we should only be laughed at."

I was then mounted behind a trooper, and we rode on into the suburbs of Munich. Here we came across a stray carriage into which I was lifted, and it was driven off to the Quatre Saisons the young officer accompanying me, whilst a trooper followed with his horse, and the others rode off to their barracks.

When we arrived, Herr Delbruck rushed so quickly down the steps to meet me, that it was apparent he had been watching within. Taking me by both hands he solicitously led me in. The officer saluted me and was turning to withdraw, when I recognized his purpose and insisted that he should come to my rooms. Over a glass of wine I warmly thanked him and his brave comrades for saving me. He replied simply that he was more than glad, and that Herr Delbruck had at the first taken steps to make all the searching party pleased; at which ambiguous utterance the maitre d'hotel smiled, while the officer pleaded duty and withdrew.

"But Herr Delbruck," I enquired, "how and why was it that the soldiers searched for me?"

He shrugged his shoulders, as if in depreciation of his own deed, as he replied, "I was so fortunate as to obtain leave from the commander of the regiment in which I serve, to ask for volunteers."

"But how did you know I was lost?" I asked.

"The driver came hither with the remains of his carriage, which had been upset when the horses ran away."

"But surely you would not send a search party of soldiers merely on this account?"

"Oh, no!" he answered, "but even before the coachman arrived, I had this telegram from the Boyar whose guest you are," and he took from his pocket a telegram which he handed to me, and I read:

Bistritz.
Be careful of my guest, his safety is most precious to me. Should aught happen to him, or if he be missed, spare nothing to find him and ensure his safety. He is English and therefore adventurous. There are often dangers from snow and wolves and night. Lose not a moment if you suspect harm to him. I answer your zeal with my fortune.
Dracula.

As I held the telegram in my hand, the room seemed to whirl around me, and if the attentive maitre d'hotel had not caught me, I think I should have fallen. There was something so strange in all this, something so weird and impossible to imagine, that there grew on me a sense of my being in some way the sport of opposite forces the mere vague idea of which seemed in a way to paralyze me. I was certainly under some form of mysterious protection. From a distant country had come, in the very nick of time, a message that took me out of the danger of the snow sleep and the jaws of the wolf.


The Burial Of The Rats

Leaving Paris by the Orleans road, cross the Enceinte, and, turning to the right, you find yourself in a somewhat wild and not at all savoury district. Right and left, before and behind, on every side rise great heaps of dust and waste accumulated by the process of time.

Paris has its night as well as its day life, and the sojourner who enters his hotel in the Rue de Rivoli or the Rue St. Honore late at night or leaves it early in the morning, can guess, in coming near Montrouge-if he has not done so already-the purpose of those great waggons that look like boilers on wheels which he finds halting everywhere as he passes.

Every city has its peculiar institutions created out of its own needs; and one of the most notable institutions of Paris is its rag-picking population. In the early morning-and Parisian life commences at an early hour-may be seen in most streets standing on the pathway opposite every court and alley and between every few houses, as still in some American cities, even in parts of New York, large wooden boxes into which the domestics or tenement-holders empty the accumulated dust of the past day. Round these boxes gather and pass on, when the work is done, to fresh fields of labour and pastures new, squalid, hungry-looking men and women, the implements of whose craft consist of a coarse bag or basket slung over the shoulder and a little rake with which they turn over and probe and examine in the minutest manner the dustbins. They pick up and deposit in their baskets, by aid of their rakes, whatever they may find, with the same facility as a Chinaman uses his chopsticks.

Paris is a city of centralisation-and centralisation and classification are closely allied. In the early times, when centralisation is becoming a fact, its forerunner is classification. All things which are similar or analogous become grouped together, and from the grouping of groups rises one whole or central point.
We see radiating many long arms with innumerable tentaculae, and in the centre rises a gigantic head with a comprehensive brain and keen eyes to look on every side and ears sensitive to hear-and a voracious mouth to swallow.

Other cities resemble all the birds and beasts and fishes whose appetites and digestions are normal. Paris alone is the analogical apotheosis of the octopus. Product of centralisation carried to an ad absurdum, it fairly represents the devil fish; and in no respects is the resemblance more curious than in the similarity of the digestive apparatus.

Those intelligent tourists who, having surrendered their individuality into the hands of Messrs. Cook or Gaze, "do" Paris in three days, are often puzzled to know how it is that the dinner which in London would cost about six shillings, can be had for three francs in a cafe in the Palais Royal. They need have no more wonder if they will but consider the classification which is a theoretic speciality of Parisian life, and adopt all round the fact from which the chiffonier has his genesis.

The Paris of 1850 was not like the Paris of to-day, and those who see the Paris of Napoleon and Baron Haussmann can hardly realise the existence of the state of things forty-five years ago.

Amongst other things, however, which have not changed are those districts where the waste is gathered. Dust is dust all the world over, in every age, and the family likeness of dust-heaps is perfect. The traveller, therefore, who visits the environs of Montrouge can go back in fancy without difficulty to the year 1850.

In this year I was making a prolonged stay in Paris. I was very much in love with a young lady who, though she returned my passion, so far yielded to the wishes of her parents that she had promised not to see me or to correspond with me for a year. I, too, had been compelled to accede to these conditions under a vague hope of parental approval. During the term of probation I had promised to remain out of the country and not to write to my dear one until the expiration of the year.

Naturally the time went heavily with me. There was no one of my own family or circle who could tell me of Alice, and none of her own folk had, I am sorry to say, sufficient generosity to send me even an occasional word of comfort regarding her health and well-being. I spent six months wandering about Europe, but as I could find no satisfactory distraction in travel, I determined to come to Paris, where, at least, I would be within easy hail of London in case any good fortune should call me thither before the appointed time. That "hope deferred maketh the heart sick" was never better exemplified than in my case, for in addition to the perpetual longing to see the face I loved there was always with me a harrowing anxiety lest some accident should prevent me showing Alice in due time that I had, throughout the long period of probation, been faithful to her trust and my own love. Thus, every adventure which I undertook had a fierce pleasure of its own, for it was fraught with possible consequences greater than it would have ordinarily borne.

Like all travellers I exhausted the places of most interest in the first month of my stay, and was driven in the second month to look for amusement whithersoever I might. Having made sundry journeys to the better-known suburbs, I began to see that there was a terra incognita, in so far as the guide book was concerned, in the social wilderness lying between these attractive points. Accordingly I began to systematise my researches, and each day took up the thread of my exploration at the place where I had on the previous day dropped it.

In process of time my wanderings led me near Montrouge, and I saw that hereabouts lay the Ultima Thule of social exploration-a country as little known as that round the source of the White Nile. And so I determined to investigate philosophically the chiffonier-his habitat, his life, and his means of life.

The job was an unsavoury one, difficult of accomplishment, and with little hope of adequate reward. However, despite reason, obstinacy prevailed, and I entered into my new investigation with a keener energy than I could have summoned to aid me in any investigation leading to any end, valuable or worthy.

One day, late in a fine afternoon, toward the end of September, I entered the holy of holies of the city of dust. The place was evidently the recognised abode of a number of chiffoniers, for some sort of arrangement was manifested in the formation of the dust heaps near the road. I passed amongst these heaps, which stood like orderly sentries, determined to penetrate further and trace dust to its ultimate location.

As I passed along I saw behind the dust heaps a few forms that flitted to and fro, evidently watching with interest the advent of any stranger to such a place.

The district was like a small Switzerland, and as I went forward my tortuous course shut out the path behind me.

Presently I got into what seemed a small city or community of chiffoniers. There were a number of shanties or huts, such as may be met with in the remote parts of the Bog of Allan-rude places with wattled walls, plastered with mud and roofs of rude thatch made from stable refuse-such places as one would not like to enter for any consideration, and which even in water-colour could only look picturesque if judiciously treated. In the midst of these huts was one of the strangest adaptations - I cannot say habitations - I had ever seen. An immense old wardrobe, the colossal remnant of some boudoir of Charles VII. or Henry II., had been converted into a dwelling-house. The double doors lay open, so that the entire ménage was open to public view. In the open half of the wardrobe was a common sitting-room of some four feet by six, in which sat, smoking their pipes round a charcoal brazier, no fewer than six old soldiers of the First Republic, with their uniforms torn and worn threadbare. Evidently they were of the mauvais sujet class; their blear eyes and limp jaws told plainly of a common love of absinthe; and their eyes had that haggard, worn look which stamps the drunkard at his worst, and that look of slumbering ferocity which follows hard in the wake of drink. The other side stood as of old, with its shelves intact, save that they were cut to half their depth, and in each shelf of which there were six, was a bed made with rags and straw. The half-dozen of worthies who inhabited this structure looked at me curiously as I passed; and when I looked back after going a little way I saw their heads together in a whispered conference. I did not like the look of this at all, for the place was very lonely, and the men looked very, very villainous. However, I did not see any cause for fear, and went on my way, penetrating further and further into the Sahara.

The way was tortuous to a degree, and from going round in a series of semi-circles, as one goes in skating with the Dutch roll, I got rather confused with regard to the points of the compass.

When I had penetrated a little way I saw, as I turned the corner of a half-made heap, sitting on a heap of straw an old soldier with threadbare coat.

"Hallo!" said I to myself; "the First Republic is well represented here in its soldiery."

As I passed him the old man never even looked up at me, but gazed on the ground with stolid persistency. Again I remarked to myself: "See what a life of rude warfare can do! This old man's curiosity is a thing of the past."

When I had gone a few steps, however, I looked back suddenly, and saw that curiosity was not dead, for the veteran had raised his head and was regarding me with a very queer expression. He seemed to me to look very like one of the six worthies in the press. When he saw me looking he dropped his head; and without thinking further of him I went on my way, satisfied that there was a strange likeness between these old warriors.

Presently I met another old soldier in a similar manner. He, too, did not notice me whilst I was passing.

By this time it was getting late in the afternoon, and I began to think of retracing my steps. Accordingly I turned to go back, but could see a number of tracks leading between different mounds and could not ascertain which of them I should take. In my perplexity I wanted to see someone of whom to ask the way, but could see no one. I determined to go on a few mounds further and so try to see someone-not a veteran.

I gained my object, for after going a couple of hundred yards I saw before me a single shanty such as I had seen before - with, however, the difference that this was not one for living in, but merely a roof with three walls open in front. From the evidences which the neighbourhood exhibited I took it to be a place for sorting. Within it was an old woman wrinkled and bent with age; I approached her to ask the way.

She rose as I came close and I asked her my way. She immediately commenced a conversation; and it occurred to me that here in the very centre of the Kingdom of Dust was the place to gather details of the history of Parisian rag-picking, particularly as I could do so from the lips of one who looked like the oldest inhabitant. I began my inquiries, and the old woman gave me most interesting answers, she had been one of the ceteuces who sat daily before the guillotine and had taken an active part among the women who signalised themselves by their violence in the revolution. While we were talking she said suddenly: "But m'sieur must be tired standing," and dusted a rickety old stool for me to sit down. I hardly liked to do so for many reasons; but the poor old woman was so civil that I did not like to run the risk of hurting her by refusing, and moreover the conversation of one who had been at the taking of the Bastille was so interesting that I sat down and so our conversation went on.

While we were talking an old man-older and more bent and wrinkled even than the woman-appeared from behind the shanty. "Here is Pierre," said she. "M'sieur can hear stories now if he wishes, for Pierre was in everything, from the Bastille to Waterloo." The old man took another stool at my request and we plunged into a sea of revolutionary reminiscences. This old man, albeit clothed like a scare-crow, was like any one of the six veterans.

I was now sitting in the centre of the low hut with the woman on my left hand and the man on my right, each of them being somewhat in front of me. The place was full of all sorts of curious objects of lumber, and of many things that I wished far away. In one corner was a heap of rags which seemed to move from the number of vermin it contained, and in the other a heap of bones whose odour was something shocking. Every now and then, glancing at the heaps, I could see the gleaming eyes of some of the rats which infested the place. These loathsome objects were bad enough, but what looked even more dreadful was an old butcher's axe with an iron handle stained with clots of blood leaning up against the wall on the right hand side. Still these things did not give me much concern. The talk of the two old people was so fascinating that I stayed on and on, till the evening came and the dust heaps threw dark shadows over the vales between them.

After a time I began to grow uneasy, I could not tell how or why, but somehow I did not feel satisfied. Uneasiness is an instinct and means warning.

The psychic faculties are often the sentries of the intellect; and when they sound alarm the reason begins to act, although perhaps not consciously.

This was so with me. I began to bethink me where I was and by what surrounded, and to wonder how I should fare in case I should be attacked; and then the thought suddenly burst upon me, although without any overt cause, that I was in danger. Prudence whispered: "Be still and make no sign," and so I was still and made no sign, for I knew that four cunning eyes were on me. "Four eyes - if not more." My God, what a horrible thought! The whole shanty might be surrounded on three sides with villains! I might be in the midst of a band of such desperadoes as only half a century of periodic revolution can produce.

With a sense of danger my intellect and observation quickened, and I grew more watchful than was my wont. I noticed that the old woman's eyes were constantly wandering toward my hands. I looked at them too, and saw the cause-my rings. On my left little finger I had a large signet and on the right a good diamond.

I thought that if there was any danger my first care was to avert suspicion. Accordingly I began to work the conversation round to rag-picking-to the drains-of the things found there; and so by easy stages to jewels. Then, seizing a favourable opportunity, I asked the old woman if she knew anything of such things. She answered that she did, a little. I held out my right hand, and, showing her the diamond, asked her what she thought of that. She answered that her eyes were bad, and stooped over my hand. I said as nonchalantly as I could: "Pardon me! You will see better thus!" and taking it off handed it to her. An unholy light came into her withered old face, as she touched it. She stole one glance at me swift and keen as a flash of lightning.

She bent over the ring for a moment, her face quite concealed as though examining it. The old man looked straight out of the front of the shanty before him, at the same time fumbling in his pockets and producing a screw of tobacco in a paper and a pipe, which he proceeded to fill. I took advantage of the pause and the momentary rest from the searching eyes on my face to look carefully round the place, now dim and shadowy in the gloaming. There still lay all the heaps of varied reeking foulness; there the terrible blood-stained axe leaning against the wall in the right hand corner, and everywhere, despite the gloom, the baleful glitter of the eyes of the rats. I could see them even through some of the chinks of the boards at the back low down close to the ground. But stay! these latter eyes seemed more than usually large and bright and baleful!

For an instant my heart stood still, and I felt in that whirling condition of mind in which one feels a sort of spiritual drunkenness, and as though the body is only maintained erect in that there is no time for it to fall before recovery. Then, in another second, I was calm-coldly calm, with all my energies in full vigour, with a self-control which I felt to be perfect and with all my feeling and instincts alert.

Now I knew the full extent of my danger: I was watched and surrounded by desperate people! I could not even guess at how many of them were lying there on the ground behind the shanty, waiting for the moment to strike. I knew that I was big and strong, and they knew it, too.

They knew also, as I did, that I was an Englishman and would make a fight for it; and so we waited. I had, I felt, gained an advantage in the last few seconds, for I knew my danger and understood the situation. Now, I thought, is the test of my courage-the enduring test: the fighting test may come later!

The old woman raised her head and said to me in a satisfied kind of way:

"A very fine ring, indeed-a beautiful ring! Oh, me! I once had such rings, plenty of them, and bracelets and earrings! Oh! for in those fine days I led the town a dance! But they've forgotten me now! They've forgotten me! They? Why they never heard of me! Perhaps their grandfathers remember me, some of them!" and she laughed a harsh, croaking laugh. And then I am bound to say that she astonished me, for she handed me back the ring with a certain suggestion of old-fashioned grace which was not without its pathos.

The old man eyed her with a sort of sudden ferocity, half rising from his stool, and said to me suddenly and hoarsely:

"Let me see!"

I was about to hand the ring when the old woman said:

"No! no, do not give it to Pierre! Pierre is eccentric. He loses things; and such a pretty ring!"

"Cat!" said the old man, savagely. Suddenly the old woman said, rather more loudly than was necessary:

"Wait! I shall tell you something about a ring." There was something in the sound other voice that jarred upon me. Perhaps it was my hyper-sensitiveness, wrought up as I was to such a pitch of nervous excitement, but I seemed to think that she was not addressing me. As I stole a glance round the place I saw the eyes of the rats in the bone heaps, but missed the eyes along the back. But even as I looked I saw them again appear. The old woman's "Wait!" had given me a respite from attack, and the men had sunk back to their reclining posture.

"I once lost a ring - a beautiful diamond hoop that had belonged to a queen, and which was given to me by a farmer of the taxes, who afterwards cut his throat because I sent him away. I thought it must have been stolen, and taxed my people; but I could get no trace.

The police came and suggested that it had found its way to the drain. We descended - I in my fine clothes, for I would not trust them with my beautiful ring! I know more of the drains since then, and of rats, too! but I shall never forget the horror of that place-alive with blazing eyes, a wall of them just outside the light of our torches. Well, we got beneath my house. We searched the outlet of the drain, and there in the filth found my ring, and we came out.

"But we found something else also before we came! As we were coming toward the opening a lot of sewer rats-human ones this time-came toward us. They told the police that one of their number had gone into the drain, but had not returned. He had gone in only shortly before we had, and, if lost, could hardly be far off. They asked help to seek him, so we turned back. They tried to prevent me going, but I insisted. It was a new excitement, and had I not recovered my ring?

Not far did we go till we came on something. There was but little water, and the bottom of the drain was raised with brick, rubbish, and much matter of the kind. He had made a fight for it, even when his torch had gone out. But they were too many for him! They had not been long about it! The bones were still warm; but they were picked clean. They had even eaten their own dead ones and there were bones of rats as well as of the man. They took it cool enough those other-the human ones-and joked of their comrade when they found him dead, though they would have helped him living. Bah! what matters it-life or death?"

"And had you no fear?" I asked her.

"Fear!" she said with a laugh. "Me have fear? Ask Pierre! But I was younger then, and, as I came through that horrible drain with its wall of greedy eyes, always moving with the circle of the light from the torches, I did not feel easy. I kept on before the men, though! It is a way I have! I never let the men get it before me. All I want is a chance and a means! And they ate him up - took every trace away except the bones; and no one knew it, nor no sound of him was ever heard!" Here she broke into a chuckling fit of the ghastliest merriment which it was ever my lot to hear and see. A great poetess describes her heroine singing: "Oh! to see or hear her singing! Scarce I know which is the divinest."

And I can apply the same idea to the old crone - in all save the divinity, for I scarce could tell which was the most hellish – the harsh, malicious, satisfied, cruel laugh, or the leering grin, and the horrible square opening of the mouth like a tragic mask, and the yellow gleam of the few discoloured teeth in the shapeless gums.

In that laugh and with that grin and the chuckling satisfaction I knew as well as if it had been spoken to me in words of thunder that my murder was settled, and the murderers only bided the proper time for its accomplishment. I could read between the lines of her gruesome story the commands to her accomplices. "Wait," she seemed to say, "bide your time. I shall strike the first blow. Find the weapon for me, and I shall make the opportunity! He shall not escape! Keep him quiet, and then no one will be wiser. There will be no outcry, and the rats will do their work!"

It was growing darker and darker; the night was coming. I stole a glance round the shanty, still all the same! The bloody axe in the corner, the heaps of filth, and the eyes on the bone heaps and in the crannies of the floor.

Pierre had been still ostensibly filling his pipe; he now struck a light and began to puff away at it. The old woman said:

"Dear heart, how dark it is! Pierre, like a good lad, light the lamp!"

Pierre got up and with the lighted match in his hand touched the wick of a lamp which hung at one side of the entrance to the shanty, and which had a reflector that threw the light all over the place.  It was evidently that which was used for their sorting at night.

"Not that, stupid! Not that! The lantern!" she called out to him. He immediately blew it out, saying: "All right, mother, I'll find it," and he hustled about the left corner of the room-the old woman saying through the darkness:

"The lantern! the lantern! Oh! That is the light that is most useful to us poor folks. The lantern was the friend of the revolution! It is the friend of the chiffonier! It helps us when all else fails."

Hardly had she said the word when there was a kind of creaking of the whole place, and something was steadily dragged over the roof.

Again I seemed to read between the lines of her words. I knew the lesson of the lantern.

"One of you get on the roof with a noose and strangle him as he passes out if we fail within."

As I looked out of the opening I saw the loop of a rope outlined black against the lurid sky. I was now, indeed, beset!

Pierre was not long in finding the lantern. I kept my eyes fixed through the darkness on the old woman. Pierre struck his light, and by its flash I saw the old woman raise from the ground beside her where it had mysteriously appeared, and then hide in the folds other gown, a long sharp knife or dagger. It seemed to be like a butcher's sharpening iron fined to a keen point.

The lantern was lit.

"Bring it here, Pierre," she said. "Place it in the doorway where we can see it. See how nice it is! It shuts out the darkness from us; it is just right!"

Just right for her and her purposes! It threw all its light on my face, leaving in gloom the faces of both Pierre and the woman, who sat outside of me on each side.

I felt that the time of action was approaching; but I knew now that the first signal and movement would come from the woman, and so watched her.

I was all unarmed, but I had made up my mind what to do. At the first movement I would seize the butcher's axe in the right-hand corner and fight my way out. At least, I would die hard. I stole a glance round to fix its exact locality so that I could not fail to seize it at the first effort, for then, if ever, time and accuracy would be precious.

Good God! It was gone! All the horror of the situation burst upon me; but the bitterest thought of all was that if the issue of the terrible position should be against me Alice would infallibly suffer. Either she would believe me false-and any lover, or any one who has ever been one, can imagine the bitterness of the thought-or else she would go on loving long after I had been lost to her and to the world, so that her life would be broken and embittered, shattered with disappointment and despair. The very magnitude of the pain braced me up and nerved me to bear the dread scrutiny of the plotters.

I think I did not betray myself. The old woman was watching me as a cat does a mouse; she had her right hand hidden in the folds of her gown, clutching, I knew, that long, cruel-looking dagger.

Had she seen any disappointment in my face she would, I felt, have known that the moment had come, and would have sprung on me like a tigress, certain of taking me unprepared.

I looked out into the night, and there I saw new cause for danger. Before and around the hut were at a little distance some shadowy forms; they were quite still, but I knew that they were all alert and on guard. Small chance for me now in that direction.

Again I stole a glance round the place. In moments of great excitement and of great danger, which is excitement, the mind works very quickly, and the keenness of the faculties which depend on the mind grows in proportion. I now felt this. In an instant I took in the whole situation. I saw that the axe had been taken through a small hole made in one of the rotten boards. How rotten they must be to allow of such a thing being done without a particle of noise.

The hut was a regular murder-trap, and was guarded all around. A garroter lay on the roof ready to entangle me with his noose if I should escape the dagger of the old hag. In front the way was guarded by I know not how many watchers. And at the back was a row of desperate men-I had seen their eyes still through the crack in the boards of the floor, when last I looked-as they lay prone waiting for the signal to start erect. If it was to be ever, now for it!

As nonchalantly as I could I turned slightly on my stool so as to get my right leg well under me. Then with a sudden jump, turning my head, and guarding it with my hands, and with the fighting instinct of the knights of old, I breathed my lady's name, and hurled myself against the back wall of the hut.

Watchful as they were, the suddenness of my movement surprised both Pierre and the old woman. As I crashed through the rotten timbers I saw the old woman rise with a leap like a tiger and heard her low gasp of baffled rage. My feet lit on something that moved, and as I jumped away I knew that I had stepped on the back of one of the row of men lying on their faces outside the hut. I was torn with nails and splinters, but otherwise unhurt. Breathless I rushed up the mound in front of me, hearing as I went the dull crash of the shanty as it collapsed into a mass.

It was a nightmare climb. The mound, though but low, was awfully steep, and with each step I took the mass of dust and cinders tore down with me and gave way under my feet. The dust rose and choked me; it was sickening, foetid, awful; but my climb was, I felt, for life or death, and I struggled on. The seconds seemed hours; but the few moments I had in starting, combined with my youth and strength, gave me a great advantage, and, though several forms struggled after me in deadly silence which was more dreadful than any sound, I easily reached the top. Since then I have climbed the cone of Vesuvius, and as I struggled up that dreary steep amid the sulphurous fumes the memory of that awful night at Montrouge came back to me so vividly that I almost grew faint.

The mound was one of the tallest in the region of dust, and as I struggled to the top, panting for breath and with my heart beating like a sledge-hammer, I saw away to my left the dull red gleam of the sky, and nearer still the flashing of lights. Thank God! I knew where I was now and where lay the road to Paris!

For two or three seconds I paused and looked back. My pursuers were still well behind me, but struggling up resolutely, and in deadly silence. Beyond, the shanty was a wreck-a mass of timber and moving forms. I could see it well, for flames were already bursting out; the rags and straw had evidently caught fire from the lantern. Still silence there! Not a sound! These old wretches could die game, anyhow.

I had no time for more than a passing glance, for as I cast an eye round the mound preparatory to making my descent I saw several dark forms rushing round on either side to cut me off on my way.

It was now a race for life. They were trying to head me on my way to Paris, and with the instinct of the moment I dashed down to the right-hand side. I was just in time, for, though I came as it seemed to me down the steep in a few steps, the wary old men who were watching me turned back, and one, as I rushed by into the opening between the two mounds in front, almost struck me a blow with that terrible butcher's axe. There could surely not be two such weapons about!

Then began a really horrible chase. I easily ran ahead of the old men, and even when some younger ones and a few women joined in the hunt I easily distanced them. But I did not know the way, and I could not even guide myself by the light in the sky, for I was running away from it. I had heard that, unless of conscious purpose, hunted men turn always to the left, and so I found it now; and so, I suppose, knew also my pursuers, who were more animals than men, and with cunning or instinct had found out such secrets for themselves: for on finishing a quick spurt, after which I intended to take a moment's breathing space, I suddenly saw ahead of me two or three forms swiftly passing behind a mound to the right.

I was in the spider's web now indeed! But with the thought of this new danger came the resource of the hunted, and so I darted down the next turning to the right. I continued in this direction for some hundred yards, and then, making a turn to the left again, felt certain that I had, at any rate, avoided the danger of being surrounded.

But not of pursuit, for on came the rabble after me, steady, dogged, relentless, and still in grim silence.

In the greater darkness the mounds seemed now to be somewhat smaller than before, although-for the night was closing-they looked bigger in proportion. I was now well ahead of my pursuers, so I made a dart up the mound in front.

Oh joy of joys! I was close to the edge of this inferno of dustheaps. Away behind me the red light of Paris in the sky, and towering up behind rose the heights of Montmartre-a dim light, with here and there brilliant points like stars.

Restored to vigour in a moment, I ran over the few remaining mounds of decreasing size, and found myself on the level land beyond. Even then, however, the prospect was not inviting. All before me was dark and dismal, and I had evidently come on one of those dank, low-lying waste places which are found here and there in the neighbourhood of great cities. Places of waste and desolation, where the space is required for the ultimate agglomeration of all that is noxious, and the ground is so poor as to create no desire of occupancy even in the lowest squatter.

With eyes accustomed to the gloom of the evening, and away now from the shadows of those dreadful dust-heaps, I could see much more easily than I could a little while ago. It might have been, of course, that the glare in the sky of the lights of Paris, though the city was some miles away, was reflected here. Howsoever it was, I saw well enough to take bearings for certainly some little distance around me.

In front was a bleak, flat waste that seemed almost dead level, with here and there the dark shimmering of stagnant pools. Seemingly far off on the right, amid a small cluster of scattered lights, rose a dark mass of Fort Montrouge, and away to the left in the dim distance, pointed with stray gleams from cottage windows, the lights in the sky showed the locality of Bicetre. A moment's thought decided me to take to the right and try to reach Montrouge. There at least would be some sort of safety, and I might possibly long before come on some of the cross roads which I knew. Somewhere, not far off, must lie the strategic road made to connect the outlying chain of forts circling the city.

Then I looked back. Coming over the mounds, and outlined black against the glare of the Parisian horizon, I saw several moving figures, and still a way to the right several more deploying out between me and my destination. They evidently meant to cut me off in this direction, and so my choice became constricted; it lay now between going straight ahead or turning to the left. Stooping to the ground, so as to get the advantage of the horizon as a line of sight, I looked carefully in this direction, but could detect no sign of my enemies. I argued that as they had not guarded or were not trying to guard that point, there was evidently danger to me there already. So I made up my mind to go straight on before me.

It was not an inviting prospect, and as I went on the reality grew worse. The ground became soft and oozy, and now and again gave way beneath me in a sickening kind of way. I seemed somehow to be going down, for I saw round me places seemingly more elevated than where I was, and this in a place which from a little way back seemed dead level. I looked around, but could see none of my pursuers. This was strange, for all along these birds of the night had followed me through the darkness as well as though it was broad daylight. How I blamed myself for coming out in my light-coloured tourist suit of tweed. The silence, and my not being able to see my enemies, whilst I felt that they were watching me, grew appalling, and in the hope of some one not of this ghastly crew hearing me I raised my voice and shouted several times. There was not the slightest response; not even an echo rewarded my efforts. For a while I stood stock still and kept my eyes in one direction. On one of the rising places around me I saw something dark move along, then another, and another. This was to my left, and seemingly moving to head me off.

I thought that again I might with my skill as a runner elude my enemies at this game, and so with all my speed darted forward.

Splash!

My feet had given way in a mass of slimy rubbish, and I had fallen headlong into a reeking, stagnant pool. The water and the mud in which my arms sank up to the elbows was filthy and nauseous beyond description, and in the suddenness of my fall I had actually swallowed some of the filthy stuff, which nearly choked me, and made me gasp for breath.

Never shall I forget the moments during which I stood trying to recover myself almost fainting from the foetid odour of the filthy pool, whose white mist rose ghostlike around. Worst of all, with the acute despair of the hunted animal when he sees the pursuing pack closing on him, I saw before my eyes whilst I stood helpless the dark forms of my pursuers moving swiftly to surround me.

It is curious how our minds work on odd matters even when the energies of thought are seemingly concentrated on some terrible and pressing need. I was in momentary peril of my life: my safety depended on my action, and my choice of alternatives coming now with almost every step I took, and yet I could not but think of the strange dogged persistency of these old men. Their silent resolution, their steadfast, grim, persistency even in such a cause commanded, as well as fear, even a measure of respect. What must they have been in the vigour of their youth. I could understand now that whirlwind rush on the bridge of Arcola, that scornful exclamation of the Old Guard at Waterloo!

Unconscious cerebration has its own pleasures, even at such moments; but fortunately it does not in any way clash with the thought from which action springs.

I realised at a glance that so far I was defeated in my object, my enemies as yet had won. They had succeeded in surrounding me on three sides, and were bent on driving me off to the left-hand, where there was already some danger for me, for they had left no guard. I accepted the alternative-it was a case of Hobson's choice and run.

I had to keep the lower ground, for my pursuers were on the higher places. However, though the ooze and broken ground impeded me my youth and training made me able to hold my ground, and by keeping a diagonal line I not only kept them from gaining on me but even began to distance them. This gave me new heart and strength, and by this time habitual training was beginning to tell and my second wind had come. Before me the ground rose slightly. I rushed up the slope and found before me a waste of watery slime, with a low dyke or bank looking black and grim beyond. I felt that if I could but reach that dyke in safety I could there, with solid ground under my feet and some kind of path to guide me, find with comparative ease a way out of my troubles. After a glance right and left and seeing no one near, I kept my eyes for a few minutes to their rightful work of aiding my feet whilst I crossed the swamp. It was rough, hard work, but there was little danger, merely toil; and a short time took me to the dyke. I rushed up the slope exulting; but here again I met a new shock. On either side of me rose a number of crouching figures. From right and left they rushed at me. Each body held a rope.

The cordon was nearly complete. I could pass on neither side, and the end was near.

There was only one chance, and I took it. I hurled myself across the dyke, and escaping out of the very clutches of my foes threw myself into the stream.

At any other time I should have thought that water foul and filthy, but now it was as welcome as the most crystal stream to the parched traveller. It was a highway of safety!

My pursuers rushed after me. Had only one of them held the rope it would have been all up with me, for he could have entangled me before I had time to swim a stroke; but the many hands holding it embarrassed and delayed them, and when the rope struck the water I heard the splash well behind me. A few minutes' hard swimming took me across the stream. Refreshed with the immersion and encouraged by the escape, I climbed the dyke in comparative gaiety of spirits.

From the top I looked back. Through the darkness I saw my assailants scattering up and down along the dyke. The pursuit was evidently not ended, and again I had to choose my course. Beyond the dyke where I stood was a wild, swampy space very similar to that which I had crossed. I determined to shun such a place, and thought for a moment whether I would take up or down the dyke. I thought I heard a sound-the muffled sound of oars, so I listened, and then shouted.

No response; but the sound ceased. My enemies had evidently got a boat of some kind. As they were on the up side of me I took the down path and began to run. As I passed to the left of where I had entered the water I heard several splashes, soft and stealthy, like the sound a rat makes as he plunges into the stream, but vastly greater; and as I looked I saw the dark sheen of the water broken by the ripples of several advancing heads. Some of my enemies were swimming the stream also.

And now behind me, up the stream, the silence was broken by the quick rattle and creak of oars; my enemies were in hot pursuit. I put my best leg foremost and ran on. After a break of a couple of minutes I looked back, and by a gleam of light through the ragged clouds I saw several dark forms climbing the bank behind me. The wind had now begun to rise, and the water beside me was ruffled and beginning to break in tiny waves on the bank. I had to keep my eyes pretty well on the ground before me, lest I should stumble, for I knew that to stumble was death. After a few minutes I looked back behind me. On the dyke were only a few dark figures, but crossing the waste, swampy ground were many more. What new danger this portended I did not know-could only guess. Then as I ran it seemed to me that my track kept ever sloping away to the right.

I looked up ahead and saw that the river was much wider than before, and that the dyke on which I stood fell quite away, and beyond it was another stream on whose near bank I saw some of the dark forms now across the marsh. I was on an island of some kind.

My situation was now indeed terrible, for my enemies had hemmed me in on every side. Behind came the quickening roll of the oars, as though my pursuers knew that the end was close. Around me on every side was desolation; there was not a roof or light, as far as I could see. Far off to the right rose some dark mass, but what it was I knew not. For a moment I paused to think what I should do, not for more, for my pursuers were drawing closer. Then my mind was made up. I slipped down the bank and took to the water. I struck out straight ahead, so as to gain the current by clearing the backwater of the island for such I presume it was, when I had passed into the stream. I waited till a cloud came driving across the moon and leaving all in darkness. Then I took off my hat and laid it softly on the water floating with the stream, and a second after dived to the right and struck out under water with all my might. I was, I suppose, half a minute under water, and when I rose came up as softly as I could, and turning, looked back.

There went my light brown hat floating merrily away. Close behind it came a rickety old boat, driven furiously by a pair of oars. The moon was still partly obscured by the drifting clouds, but in the partial light I could see a man in the bows holding aloft ready to strike what appeared to me to be that same dreadful pole-axe which I had before escaped.

As I looked the boat drew closer, closer, and the man struck savagely. The hat disappeared. The man fell forward, almost out of the boat. His comrades dragged him in but without the axe, and then as I turned with all my energies bent on reaching the further bank, I heard the fierce whirr of the muttered "Sacre!" which marked the anger of my baffled pursuers.

That was the first sound I had heard from human lips during all this dreadful chase, and full as it was of menace and danger to me it was a welcome sound for it broke that awful silence which shrouded and appalled me. It was as though an overt sign that my opponents were men and not ghosts, and that with them I had, at least, the chance of a man, though but one against many.

But now that the spell of silence was broken the sounds came thick and fast. From boat to shore and back from shore to boat came quick question and answer, all in the fiercest whispers. I looked back-a fatal thing to do-for in the instant someone caught sight of my face, which showed white on the dark water, and shouted. Hands pointed to me, and in a moment or two the boat was under weigh, and following hard after me. I had but a little way to go, but quicker and quicker came the boat after me. A few more strokes and I would be on the shore, but I felt the oncoming of the boat, and expected each second to feel the crash of an oar or other weapon on my head. Had I not seen that dreadful axe disappear in the water I do not think that I could have won the shore. I heard the muttered curses of those not rowing and the laboured breath of the rowers. With one supreme effort for life or liberty I touched the bank and sprang up it. There was not a single second to spare, for hard behind me the boat grounded and several dark forms sprang after me. I gained the top of the dyke, and keeping to the left ran on again. The boat put off and followed down the stream. Seeing this I feared danger in this direction, and quickly turning, ran down the dyke on the other side, and after passing a short stretch of marshy ground gained a wild, open flat country and sped on.

Still behind me came on my relentless pursuers. Far away, below me, I saw the same dark mass as before, but now grown closer and greater. My heart gave a great thrill of delight, for I knew that it must be the fortress of Bicetre, and with new courage I ran on. I had heard that between each and all of the protecting forts of Paris there are strategic ways, deep sunk roads, where soldiers marching should be sheltered from an enemy. I knew that if I could gain this road I would be safe, but in the darkness I could not see any sign of it, so, in blind hope of striking it, I ran on. Presently I came to the edge of a deep cut, and found that down below me ran a road guarded on each side by a ditch of water fenced on either side by a straight, high wall.

Getting fainter and dizzier, I ran on; the ground got more broken-more and more still, till I staggered and fell, and rose again, and ran on in the blind anguish of the hunted. Again the thought of Alice nerved me. I would not be lost and wreck her life: I would fight and struggle for life to the bitter end. With a great effort I caught the top of the wall.

As, scrambling like a catamount, I drew myself up, I actually felt a hand touch the sole of my foot. I was now on a sort of causeway, and before me I saw a dim light. Blind and dizzy, I ran on, staggered, and fell, rising, covered with dust and blood.

"Halt la!"

The words sounded like a voice from heaven. A blaze of light seemed to enwrap me, and I shouted with joy.

"Qui va la?" The rattle of musketry, the flash of steel before my eyes.

Instinctively I stopped, though close behind me came a rush of my pursuers.

Another word or two, and out from a gateway poured, as it seemed to me, a tide of red and blue, as the guard turned out. All around seemed blazing with light, and the flash of steel, the clink and rattle of arms, and the loud, harsh voices of command. As I fell forward, utterly exhausted, a soldier caught me. I looked back in dreadful expectation, and saw the mass of dark forms disappearing into the night. Then I must have fainted. When I recovered my senses I was in the guard room. They gave me brandy, and after awhile I was able to tell them something of what had passed. Then a commissary of police appeared, apparently out of the empty air, as is the way of the Parisian police officer. He listened attentively, and then had a moment's consultation with the officer in command. Apparently they were agreed, for they asked me if I were ready now to come with them.

"Where to?" I asked, rising to go.

"Back to the dust heaps. We shall, perhaps, catch them yet!"

"I shall try!" said I.

He eyed me for a moment keenly, and said suddenly: "Would you like to wait awhile or till to-morrow, young Englishman?" This touched me to the quick, as, perhaps, he intended, and I jumped to my feet.

"Come now!" I said; "now! now! An Englishman is always ready for his duty!"

The commissary was a good fellow, as well as a shrewd one; he slapped my shoulder kindly. "Brave garcon!" he said. "Forgive me, but I knew what would do you most good. The guard is ready. Come!"

And so, passing right through the guard room, and through a long vaulted passage, we were out into the night. A few of the men in front had powerful lanterns. Through courtyards and down a sloping way we passed out through a low archway to a sunken road, the same that I had seen in my flight. The order was given to get at the double, and with a quick, springing stride, half run, half walk, the soldiers went swiftly along. I felt my strength renewed again-such is the difference between hunter and hunted.

A very short distance took us to a low-lying pontoon bridge across the stream, and evidently very little higher up than I had struck it. Some effort had evidently been made to damage it, for the ropes had all been cut, and one of the chains had been broken. I heard the officer say to the commissary:

"We are just in time! A few more minutes, and they would have destroyed the bridge. Forward, quicker still!" and on we went. Again we reached a pontoon on the winding stream; as we came up we heard the hollow boom of the metal drums as the efforts to destroy the bridge was again renewed. A word of command was given, and several men raised their rifles.

"Fire!" A volley rang out. There was a muffled cry, and the dark forms dispersed. But the evil was done, and we saw the far end of the pontoon swing into the stream. This was a serious delay, and it was nearly an hour before we had renewed ropes and restored the bridge sufficiently to allow us to cross.

We renewed the chase. Quicker, quicker we went towards the dust heaps.

After a time we came to a place that I knew. There were the remains of a fire - a few smouldering wood ashes still cast a red glow, but the bulk of the ashes were cold. I knew the site of the hut and the hill behind it up which I had rushed, and in the flickering glow the eyes of the rats still shone with a sort of phosphorescence. The commissary spoke a word to the officer, and he cried:

"Halt!"

The soldiers were ordered to spread around and watch, and then we commenced to examine the ruins. The commissary himself began to lift away the charred boards and rubbish. These the soldiers took and piled together. Presently he started back, then bent down and rising beckoned me.

"See!" he said.

It was a gruesome sight. There lay a skeleton face downwards, a woman by the lines-an old woman by the coarse fibre of the bone. Between the ribs rose a long spike-like dagger made from a butcher's sharpening knife, its keen point buried in the spine.

"You will observe," said the commissary to the officer and to me as he took out his note book, "that the woman must have fallen on her dagger. The rats are many here - see their eyes glistening among that heap of bones - and you will also notice" I shuddered as he placed his hand on the skeleton "that but little time was lost by them, for the bones are scarcely cold!"

There was no other sign of any one near, living or dead; and so deploying again into line the soldiers passed on. Presently we came to the hut made of the old wardrobe. We approached. In five of the six compartments was an old man sleeping-sleeping so soundly that even the glare of the lanterns did not wake them. Old and grim and grizzled they looked, with their gaunt, wrinkled, bronzed faces and their white moustaches.

The officer called out harshly and loudly a word of command, and in an instant each one of them was on his feet before us and standing at "attention!"

"What do you here?"

"We sleep," was the answer.

"Where are the other chiffoniers?" asked the commissary.

"Gone to work."

"And you?"

"We are on guard!"

"Peste!" laughed the officer grimly, as he looked at the old men one after the other in the face and added with cool deliberate cruelty, "Asleep on duty! Is this the manner of the Old Guard? No wonder, then, a Waterloo!"

By the gleam of the lantern I saw the grim old faces grow deadly pale, and almost shuddered at the look in the eyes of the old men as the laugh of the soldiers echoed the grim pleasantry of the officer.

I felt in that moment that I was in some measure avenged.

For a moment they looked as if they would throw themselves on the taunter, but years of their life had schooled them and they remained still.

"You are but five," said the commissary; "where is the sixth?" The answer came with a grim chuckle.

"He is there!" and the speaker pointed to the bottom of the wardrobe. "He died last night. You won't find much of him. The burial of the rats is quick!"

The commissary stooped and looked in. Then he turned to the officer and said calmly:

"We may as well go back. No trace here now; nothing to prove that man was the one wounded by your soldiers' bullets! Probably they murdered him to cover up the trace. See!" again he stooped and placed his hands on the skeleton. "The rats work quickly and they are many. These bones are warm!"

I shuddered, and so did many more of those around me.

"Form!" said the officer, and so in marching order, with the lanterns swinging in front and the manacled veterans in the midst, with steady tramp we took ourselves out of the dust-heaps and turned backward to the fortress of Bicetre.

My year of probation has long since ended, and Alice is my wife. But when I look back upon that trying twelvemonth one of the most vivid incidents that memory recalls is that associated with my visit to the City of Dust.

www.ingramcontent.com/pod-product-compliance
Lightning Source LLC
Chambersburg PA
CBHW071353130626
46556CB00005B/2172